The Dragonsitter's Castle

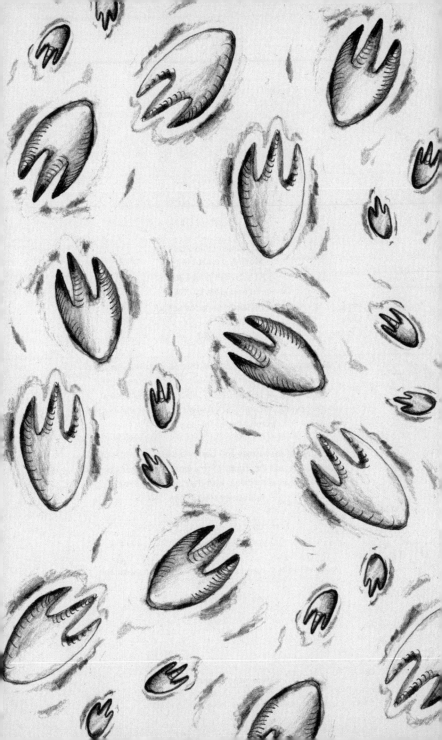

First published in 2013 by
Andersen Press Limited
20 Vauxhall Bridge Road
London SW1V 2SA
www.andersenpress.co.uk

6 8 10 9 7

British Library Cataloguing in Publication Data available.

ISBN 978 1 84939 769 8

Printed and bound in Malta

The Dragonsitter's Castle

Josh Lacey

Illustrated by Garry Parsons

Andersen Press
London

From: Edward Smith-Pickle

To: Morton Pickle

Date: Monday 26 December

Subject: Look who's here

Attachments: Unexpected guests

Dear Uncle Morton

I just tried calling you, but the phone made a funny noise. Have you changed your number?

I wanted to tell you your dragons are here.

They must have arrived in the middle of the night. When I came down for breakfast, Ziggy was sitting on the patio, peering through the window, looking very sorry for herself.

I didn't even see baby Arthur. I thought Ziggy had left him at home. Then I realised he was tucked under her tummy, trying to keep warm.

They're feeling better now we've given them some toast and let them sit by the radiator.

1

Have they come to say Happy Christmas?
Are you coming too? I'm afraid we haven't
got you a present, but there's lots of turkey
left and about a million brussels sprouts.

Love from

Eddie

Dear Uncle Morton

Your dragons are still here. They have eaten the entire contents of the fridge and most of the tins in the cupboard too.

Arthur also swallowed three spoons and the remote control.

Mum says they will probably come out the other end, but I'm not really looking forward to that.

She wants to know when you are coming to collect the dragons.

We're leaving first thing on Thursday morning, so she says could you get here by Wednesday afternoon at the latest?

Eddie

From: Edward Smith-Pickle

To: Morton Pickle

Date: Wednesday 28 December

Subject: Please call us!

Dear Uncle Morton

Your phone is still making the same noise. Mum says you've probably been cut off because you haven't paid your bill.

Does that mean you haven't got my emails either?

So what are we supposed to do with the dragons?

We're leaving first thing tomorrow morning.

Mum has to catch the 9.03 or she won't arrive in time for the meet-and-greet with Swami Ticklemore.

She is going on that yoga retreat like you suggested. She says she deserves it after the year she's had.

I asked if the dragons could stay here without us, but she said no way, José, which you have to admit is fair enough after last time.

Emily and I are going to stay with Dad in his new house. He says it's a castle, but Dad's always saying things like that.

I rang him and asked if we could bring the dragons.

He said no, because his new girlfriend Bronwen is allergic to fur.

I told him dragons don't have fur, but he said even so.

So please come and get them ASAP.

Eddie

PS I've been waiting with my rubber gloves, but there's still no sign of those spoons or the remote control.

Dear Uncle Morton

Mum says if you're not here in the next ten minutes, she'll leave the dragons in the street and they can take care of themselves.

I said you couldn't possibly get from Scotland to here in ten minutes, and she said worse things happen at sea.

I have literally no idea what she meant.

Now she and Dad are shouting at one another just like they used to when they were still married.

If you get this in the next ten minutes, please call us!

Eddie

From: Edward Smith–Pickle

To: Morton Pickle

Date: Thursday 29 December

Subject: Don't go to our house!

Attachments: Car; castle

Dear Uncle Morton

I hope you haven't left already to pick up the dragons, because they're not at our house any more.

Dad said they could come to his castle after all.

I don't know what changed his mind, but he did say the Welsh have always had a soft spot for dragons.

Luckily Bronwen had stayed behind, so there was room for all five of us in the car.

Dad was worried about his seats, but I told him dragons can be very careful with their claws if they want to, and I'm glad to say they were.

We got a lot of strange looks on the motorway, and there was a nasty moment when Arthur flapped his wings and almost got sucked out of the window, but now we've arrived at Dad's new castle, and we're all fine.

It really is a castle!

There's a moat and half a drawbridge and a
rusty old cannon by the front door.

Dad bought it cheap because the previous
owner had lost all his money.

He is going to convert it into apartments and sell them off and finally make his millions.

Our bedroom is in a turret. There's a little wooden staircase which goes to the top and you can see for miles.

The only problem is it's freezing. Dad says that's the price you have to pay for living in a historical building, but I don't see why he couldn't just buy some heaters.

Here is the address:

Manawydan Castle,
Llefelys,
Near Llandrindod Wells,
Powys, Wales

Dad says please come and pick up the dragons ASAP because he and Bronwen are having a party on New Year's Eve and they want everything to go perfectly.

Eddie

Dear Uncle Morton

I forgot to say: please bring some medicine for Ziggy.

She's got a terrible cold.

When she sneezes, little jets of fire come out of her nostrils. I hope it's not contagious.

Eddie

Hi Eddie

I'm very sorry that I haven't replied before, but my communication with the outside world has been severed for more than a week by the thick layer of snow smothering my island. I even had to dig a path from my back door to the shed so I could bring back some dry logs for the fire.

My boat was frozen solid, so I couldn't possibly get to the mainland, and I spent the festive season alone, reading several excellent books and eating my way through whatever I could find at the back of my cupboard. Luckily I had stocked up on my last trip to France, so I spent a very happy Christmas eating duck paté and drinking some wonderful red wine.

The dragons weren't so content. They huddled by the fire for the first couple of days, then disappeared. How very sensible of them to come and find you.

I polished off the last of my tins last night and raised a red flag. Luckily Mr McDougall saw it first thing this morning and came to rescue me in his boat.

I'm now checking my emails in his house.
He sends Season's Greetings, by the way,
and hopes to meet you soon.

I'm sorry to hear that Ziggy is unwell.
Please try to keep her and Arthur
comfortable until I arrive. I wouldn't want
them to fly any further south. They'd only
get lost.

Mr McDougall's nephew Gordon is giving
me a lift to the train station. I have just
checked the timetables. If I make my
connections at Glasgow and Crewe,
I should be with you tonight.

With lots of love from your affectionate
uncle

Morton

From: Edward Smith–Pickle

To: Morton Pickle

Date: Friday 30 December

Subject: Champagne

Attachments: Snowdragon

Dear Uncle Morton

We're all very glad you're coming!

We're going out now to pick up the drinks for the party, but we'll be back by six o'clock.

If you get here early, Dad says the pub in the village is excellent, although he advises against the pickled eggs.

Bronwen says please don't bring any more snow, because we've got enough already. It came down last night and we're now knee-deep.

We just went out to make a snowman, but we made something much better instead. Here's a picture. Can you guess what it is?

Arthur jumped around all over the place, making funny little barking noises, then challenged the snowdragon to a duel.

He melted a hole in its middle, which made him even more confused.

If the snow hasn't gone in the morning, will you help us make another?

Eddie

From: Edward Smith–Pickle
To: Morton Pickle
Date: Friday 30 December
Subject: Medicine
Attachments: Hottie

Dear Uncle Morton

I'm really sorry. Arthur has caught his mum's cold.

It's my fault. I shouldn't have let him play in the snow.

I've given them hot water bottles, but they won't stop sneezing.

I hope you're bringing lots of medicine.

Eddie

Dear Uncle Morton

We're going to bed now, but Dad will leave the door unlocked. We've made up a bed for you on the sofa in the sitting room, which is actually the warmest room in the castle.

I asked if you could stay for the party, but Dad said only without the dragons, so I suppose that means no.

I wish you could. It really is going to be a great party.

We've been helping Bronwen make the canapés. There's smoked salmon and mini pizzas and cheese straws and chicken wings, plus enough crisps to fill twelve huge bowls.

Bronwen wants us to take everyone's coats
when they arrive. Dad has bought about a
million fireworks to set off at midnight.

Dad says we can stay up to watch. I reminded him that Emily is only five, but he said it would be good for her.

I said Mum would be furious, and he said she'd be furious whatever he did, which is probably true.

Eddie

Dear Uncle Morton

Are you stuck in a snowdrift?

I hope not, because Dad is going to evict the dragons if you're not here by lunchtime.

I said he can't make sick dragons sleep outside in this weather, and he said hard cheese.

Eddie

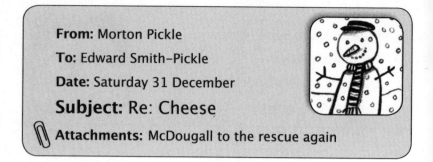

From: Morton Pickle

To: Edward Smith-Pickle

Date: Saturday 31 December

Subject: Re: Cheese

Attachments: McDougall to the rescue again

Sorry about delay. Helping McD rescue
sheep from unexpected avalanche.

Gordon taking me to station now.

With you 4pm at latest.

M

From: Edward Smith–Pickle

To: Morton Pickle

Date: Saturday 31 December

Subject: Canapés

Attachments: Crime scene

Dear Uncle Morton

Could you try to get here before 4pm? The dragons have ruined the party, so we have to leave the castle right now.

It happened when we came back from making the second snowdragon. I was just taking off my boots when I heard a terrible scream. I thought Emily must have seen another mouse. I ran into the kitchen and found a scene of total devastation.

There were vol-au-vents everywhere. The floor was covered with crisps. Somehow twenty miniature Scotch eggs had got stuck to the ceiling. The entire platter of smoked salmon had gone, including all six lemons and the pepper grinder.

Bronwen said she'd only nipped outside for a second to fetch another jar of mayonnaise, but she must have been gone for longer than that, because not even Ziggy can eat 600 canapés in one second.

I thought the dragons might at least look guilty, but I've never seen anyone looking so pleased with themselves.

The good thing is they must be getting better if they're hungry.

I didn't say that to Dad, because I could see he wasn't in the mood.

When Bronwen finally stopped shouting, she said in a quiet voice, enough is enough, and it was them or her.

Dad said he was sorry, but he hardly knew the dragons, and they were big enough to look after themselves, and then he said some things about you, Uncle Morton, which you probably don't want to know.

I said if the dragons left then I was leaving too.

Emily said so was she.

Dad told us not to be ridiculous, but we weren't.

You'll find us at the castle gates.

I hope you'll be here soon, Uncle Morton, because the forecast is more snow.

Eddie

Dear Uncle Morton

You'll be glad to hear we're back in the castle. It's not much warmer than outside, but at least we don't get covered in snow.

Dad came to get us. He made a deal with Bronwen. She doesn't mind the dragons staying if they're locked in our turret at the top of the castle. We have to stay with them till you arrive.

See you at 4pm if not before.

Eddie

Dear Uncle Morton

It's 8.20 and the first guests have just arrived.

We're still stuck in the turret with your dragons.

I said what about the coats, and Bronwen said the coats could take care of themselves.

Where are you?

E

From: Morton Pickle

To: Edward Smith-Pickle

Date: Sunday 1 January

Subject: Re: 4pm at latest?????

Hi Eddie

I'm sure you're safely tucked up in bed at this unearthly hour of the morning, but I wanted to wish you a very Happy New Year.

I'm terribly sorry that I haven't reached you yet, but the avalanche turned out to be more serious than first thought, and I've been helping Mr McDougall retrieve a hundred and eleven sheep that had been scattered around the hills.

They are all now safely in his barn. We have just celebrated midnight with a chorus of Auld Lang Syne and a magnificent single malt whisky that the McDougalls had been saving for a special occasion.

Gordon will give me a lift to the station first thing. I should be with you in time for tea.

Morton

Dear Uncle Morton

I'm very glad to hear you're finally coming to Wales, but please don't go to the castle. We're not there any more. We are staying in the Manawydan Arms in Llefelys.

You're probably wondering why we're not staying in the castle, and the reason is very simple. Ziggy burnt it down.

You can't exactly blame her (although Dad does) because she didn't mean to.

It happened last night. The four of us were in the turret, looking out of the window, watching cars pulling up and guests hurrying into the castle.

I now know you were four hundred miles

away, Uncle M, but I didn't at the time, and I kept hoping to see you.

Emily and I had our duvets, but the dragons were freezing. There was snow coming through the holes in the windows. I was worried the two poor shivering dragons would get pneumonia.

Then I had a great idea. Our room had a fireplace. Why didn't we use it?

I sneaked downstairs and grabbed some wood and a newspaper. Dad had taught me how to scrunch up the paper and make a pyramid from the kindling. He did tell me never to light a fire without adult supervision, but we were so cold I had to do something. I was just looking round for some matches when Ziggy sneezed and the whole pile burst into flames.

For a moment we were lovely and warm.

Then a rocket whooshed past my left ear and exploded against the ceiling.

Someone must have left a box of fireworks in the kindling basket. Maybe I picked some up by mistake when I was gathering wood. They do look very like ordinary sticks.

Another rocket shot across the room and through the window, smashing the one

pane of glass that wasn't already broken.

A Catherine Wheel span across the floor and down the stairs.

One of the fireworks must have set fire to a curtain or a duvet, and suddenly the turret was in flames.

Emily screamed so loudly I thought my eardrums might burst. I was trying to stay calm, but I was beginning to panic too. It was extremely hot and quite difficult to breathe, and our route downstairs was blocked by a thick wall of black smoke.

There was only one way out.

We had to go up.

We charged to the top of the turret, followed by the dragons. Fireworks were exploding in every direction. Down on the ground, I could see guests flooding out of the castle.

We screamed for help, but no one could hear us.

Luckily Ziggy knew what to do. She bent her neck and flapped her wings.

All three of us hopped aboard.

When we took off, there was a huge cheer from all Dad's guests. They must have thought we were part of the display.

I had expected Ziggy to land beside Dad,
but she flew into the woods and landed
under a big tree.

Once she was on the ground, she refused to
move. She and Arthur just curled up in the
snow. I said it wasn't a sensible place for a
snooze if you've got a cold, but they took
no notice.

Emily and I had to walk home. We were both shivering. Emily's lips turned blue.

Just when I thought we might die of frostbite, I heard someone shouting our names. I shouted back. It was Dad. He came running through the trees and gathered us both up in his arms and said he'd thought we were dead. I'd never seen him cry before.

The fire had died down by the time we got back to the castle. Dad gave the firemen a crate of champagne to say thank you. The labels had burnt off the bottles, but they didn't mind.

Emily and I are sharing a room in the Manawydan Arms. Dad is asleep next door. He's probably going to kill me when he wakes up.

I wish I could say Happy New Year, but it really isn't.

Eddie

From: Edward Smith-Pickle

To: Morton Pickle

Date: Monday 2 January

Subject: Unhappy New Year

Attachments: The ruins

Dear Uncle Morton

I don't know where you are or what's happened you, but if you do ever get here, we are still staying at the Manawydan Arms. It's the only pub in the village and Dad says you can't miss it.

The three of us went back to the castle today. There's not much left, just a few blackened walls and some smouldering timbers.

In case you're wondering why there are only three of us, Bronwen has gone to her mother's in Aberystwyth. She and Dad had a big row last night.

Bronwen said sorry to me and Emily for her

language, but I said she shouldn't worry, we'd heard it all before when Mum and Dad were getting divorced, and worse too.

Bronwen said Dad obviously hadn't learned from his mistakes, and he said she was right about that. That was when she left.

There's still no sign of the dragons. Dad says they're old enough to look after themselves, but Arthur certainly isn't, and I'm not sure if Ziggy is either, especially when she's got a cold.

Also Dad says I owe him a new castle.

I thought he was joking, but he's not.

Apparently he borrowed all the money to buy the castle, and now he'll never be able to pay it back.

He's ruined, and it's my fault.

Today is only the second of January, but this is already turning out to be the worst year of my life.

Eddie

From: Edward Smith-Pickle
To: Morton Pickle
Date: Tuesday 3 January
Subject: Lost

Dear Uncle Morton

I'm a terrible dragonsitter. There's still no sign of Ziggy or Arthur, and I have no idea where they might be.

There's no sign of Bronwen either, but Dad said not to worry about her, because there are lots more fish in the sea.

Emily said he could get married to Mum again, but Dad said he'd been married to her once already and that was enough for any man.

Dad is going back to the castle today. Emily and I are going with him, and we'll search the forest for your dragons.

Eddie

Dear Eddie

I'm terribly sorry to hear about the castle.
Please pass on my apologies to your father.
I don't have the funds to pay for a new
castle, but I will help in any way that I can.

I'm sorry that I haven't reached you yet,
but there has been a crisis in the village.
The weight of snow on the church roof
caused it to collapse. Mr McDougall and I,
along with all other able-bodied men and
women, have been called upon to help.

You will be glad to hear we have now
repaired the worst of the damage. I'm
going to the station now and shall be
with you this afternoon.

Don't worry about Ziggy and Arthur. I have read that the caves of North Wales were once full of dragons, so they have probably sniffed out some distant relatives. We shall search for them together when I arrive.

Morton

Dear Uncle Morton

We have reserved a room for you at the Manawydan Arms.

It's Quiz Night tonight and there's a prize of a hundred pounds, which would be really useful now I'm saving up to buy a new castle.

If you get here in time, you could join our team. I bet you're brilliant at quizzes.

We spent today at the castle again, but there's still no sign of your dragons. I hope you're right about them hiding in a cave. I'm just worried they won't be warm enough.

Eddie

From: Morton Pickle
To: Edward Smith-Pickle
Date: Thursday 5 January
Subject: Re: Quiz Night

Delayed again. Leaving now.

Sorry to miss quiz.

M

Dear Uncle Morton

The Manawydan Arms is full. They won't reserve a room for you, because you didn't use the one they kept for you yesterday, but you can sleep on the floor in ours.

Dad is driving us home first thing tomorrow morning, so you can keep the room if you want to stay here while you search for the dragons.

Don't worry about missing Quiz Night. We came second and won a prize of fifty pounds!

When I told Dad I would add it to his savings for a new castle, he told me not to be ridiculous and bought a round of drinks for everyone in the pub.

I suppose that's what Mum means about him being useless with money.

He had a piece of good news yesterday, so there was something to celebrate. The man from the insurance company thinks his policy should pay out in full because the fire was caused by misadventure and/or faulty equipment.

Emily told him that the fire was actually caused by a dragon trying to keep warm.

The insurance man said he'd never heard that one before.

Dad gave me a look, so I kept quiet, and we pretended Emily has a vivid imagination.

See you later.

Eddie

From: Morton Pickle

To: Edward Smith–Pickle

Date: Friday 6 January

Subject: Re: Our last night

Attachments: Home sweet home

Dear Eddie

I hope you're safely home by now. I'm terribly sorry that I never reached Wales and didn't get a chance to see your father's castle. However, it all turns out to have been for the best.

I was finally ready to catch a train yesterday when I remembered that you had asked me to bring some medicine. I have a large stock in my bathroom cabinet, so I borrowed Mr McDougall's boat and whizzed across the channel to my island.

I moored the boat and hurried up the path to the house, and was just reaching for my keys when who should I see lounging on the lawn. . .

There they were, my two dragons, enjoying this morning's unexpected sunshine. They showed no shame for causing so much trouble. All they wanted was a snack and a belly-rub, and happily I was able to provide both.

You'll be glad to hear that their coughs and colds are entirely cured. I'm sorry they didn't behave themselves, but thanks again for looking after them so well.

Perhaps this year you will finally come and visit us?

Love from

Morton, Ziggy and Arthur

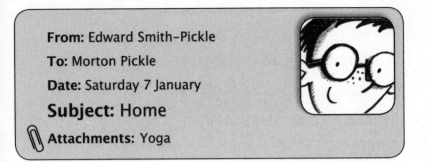

From: Edward Smith-Pickle

To: Morton Pickle

Date: Saturday 7 January

Subject: Home

Attachments: Yoga

Dear Uncle Morton

I'm very pleased the dragons are safe. I was getting quite worried they might never be found.

We're home too and everything is fine.

Mum says THANK YOU for recommending the ashram. (She asked me to put that in capital letters.) She says she's never felt so relaxed in her entire life.

It's true. She didn't even mind about the burn marks on our pyjamas.

She wants to go back ASAP, so maybe I could come and stay then?

Happy New Year!

And lots of love

from your favourite nephew

Eddie

PS Will you keep looking in Arthur's poos? Mum says the spoons don't matter, but it would be good if we could turn on the telly.

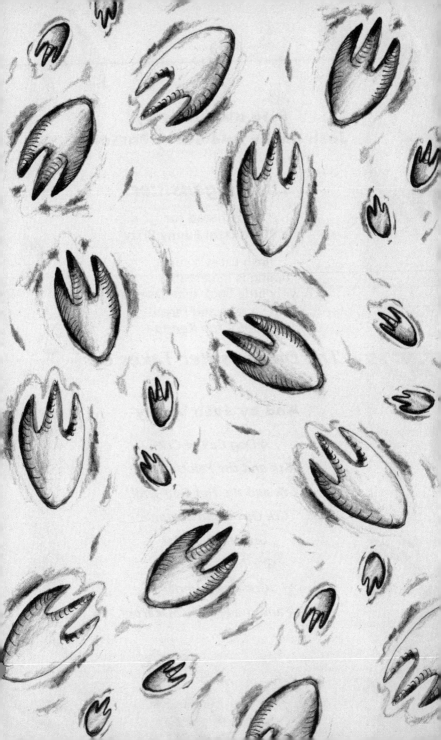

Also available by
Josh Lacey and Garry Parsons:

The Dragonsitter

**Shortlisted for
the Roald Dahl Funny Prize**

'Josh Lacey's comic
timing is impeccable . . .
A witty little book that deserves
to be read and reread'
Books for Keeps

The Dragonsitter Takes Off

And by Josh Lacey:

A Dog Called Grk

Grk and the Pelotti Gang

Grk and the Hot Dog Trail

Grk Operation Tortoise

Grk Smells a Rat

Grk Takes Revenge

Grk Down Under

Grk and the Phoney Macaroni